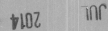

A PIECE OF CAKE

by LeUyen Pham

BALZER + BRAY
An Imprint of HarperCollins Publishers

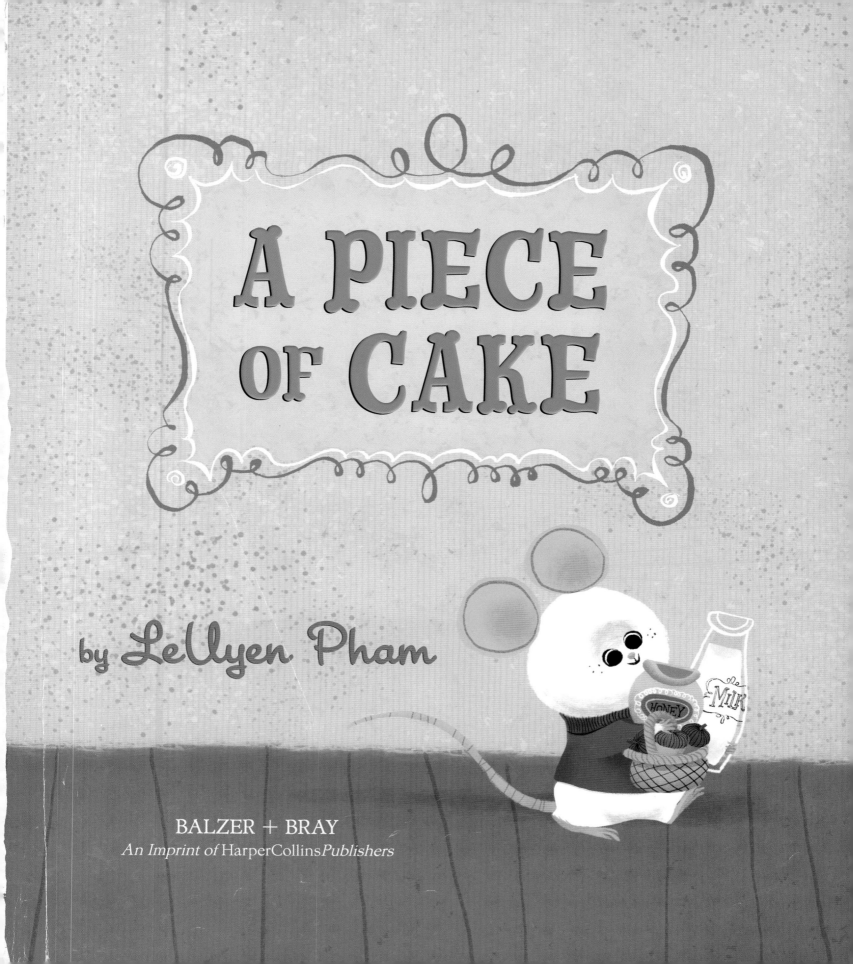

It was Little Bird's birthday. Mouse, who was a very kind mouse, made her a cake.

He worked the whole morning through and used up everything in his pantry.

Mouse began to walk to Little Bird's home.
On the way, he met Chicken, sitting with all her eggs.

Hello, Chicken!

said Mouse.

Chicken said,

Yummers, that's one tasty-looking cake!
Hey, Mouse, could I have some?
If you give me a piece of that cake,
I'll trade you . . .

Mouse didn't think Little Bird would need a cork.

But Mouse was a very kind mouse.

Surely Little Bird would
not mind if I gave
Chicken some of her cake.

So Mouse traded one piece of cake
for the cork and went on his way.

Next, Mouse met Squirrel, who was gathering nuts.

Hello, Squirrel!

said Mouse.

Squirrel said,

Gadzooks, that's one tasty-looking cake!
Mouse, old buddy, how about giving
me some? If you give me a piece of cake,
I'll trade you . . .

NUTS
for
NUTS

Mouse couldn't imagine that Little Bird would need a wire.

But Mouse was a very kind mouse.

Surely Little Bird would
not mind if I gave
Squirrel some of her cake.

So Mouse traded one piece of cake
for the wire and went on his way.

Soon, Mouse met Bear,
surrounded by his many
pots of honey.

Hello, Bear!

said Mouse.

Bear said,

Wowsers, that's one tasty-looking cake! Mouse, my fine little fellow, would you mind giving me some? If you give me a piece of cake, I'll trade you . . .

Mouse was *sure* that Little Bird did not want a net.

But Mouse was a very kind mouse.

Surely Little Bird would
not mind if I gave
Bear some of her cake.

So Mouse traded one piece
of cake for the net and
went on his way.

Farther on, Mouse met Cow, who
was surrounded by bottles of milk.

Hello, Cow!

said Mouse.

But Mouse was a very kind mouse.

Surely Little Bird would
not mind if I gave
Cow some of her cake.

So Mouse traded the last
piece of cake for the flyswatter
and went on his way.

Finally, he reached Little Bird's house.

Oh, Little Bird! I wanted to bring you a cake for your birthday. But I traded the pieces of cake for a cork, a wire, a net, and a flyswatter. I would make you another cake, but I've used up everything in my pantry.

I'm so sorry.

But Little Bird, who was
a very clever bird, said,

Oh, but Mouse! These are
wonderful presents! Come
with me and I'm sure
we'll find a use for them.

First, they met Cow.

What's wrong, Cow?

asked Mouse.

I lost the cap to my soap bottle. If only I had something to cork it up with. . . .

Well,

said clever Little Bird,

Cow, my dear, if you give us some milk, we'll give you . . .

And Little Bird twisted the wire into a loop, dipped it into the soap, and blew bubbles.

WOW! said Cow.

So Cow traded the milk for the wire, and Mouse and Little Bird went on their way.

Next, they met Bear.

What's wrong,
Bear?

asked Mouse.

These bees won't leave me alone! If only I had something to swat them away.

Well, said clever Little Bird,

Bear, my fine fellow, if you give us some honey, we'll give you . . .

HONEY
HONEY
HONEY
HONEY
HONEY
EY

And Little Bird popped the cork into the hive to keep the bees from coming out.

Excellent!

said Bear.

So Bear traded the honey for the cork, and Mouse and Little Bird went on their way.

Soon, they ran
into Squirrel.

What's wrong, Squirrel?

asked Mouse.

I can't get my nuts into
the tree! If only I had
something to carry
them up with.

Well,

said clever Little Bird,

Squirrel, my friend, if you give us some nuts, we'll give you . . .

And Little Bird bent the flyswatter in the ground, loaded it with nuts, and let it go. The nuts flew through the air and landed in the nest.

Cool!

said Squirrel.

So Squirrel traded some nuts for the flyswatter, and Mouse and Little Bird went on their way.

Finally, they met Chicken.

What's wrong, Chicken?

I dropped the piece of cake Mouse gave me. Oh, if only I had another piece to eat!

Oh, dear. . . .

"Well," said kind Mouse, "Chicken, dear Chicken, if you give us some eggs, we'll give you . . ."

an INVITATION!

An invitation?

Yes! To Little Bird's birthday party! With your eggs, Squirrel's nuts, Bear's honey, and Cow's milk, we can make another cake. Invite everyone, and we can each have a piece of cake!

Yay! said Chicken.

So Chicken traded two eggs for the invitation and ran off to tell the others.

And Mouse and Little Bird went on to Mouse's home.

Mouse and Little Bird worked all that
afternoon, and together they made a
cake that looked and tasted even better
than the first one.

After everyone was given a piece,
Mouse gave Little Bird
one last present.

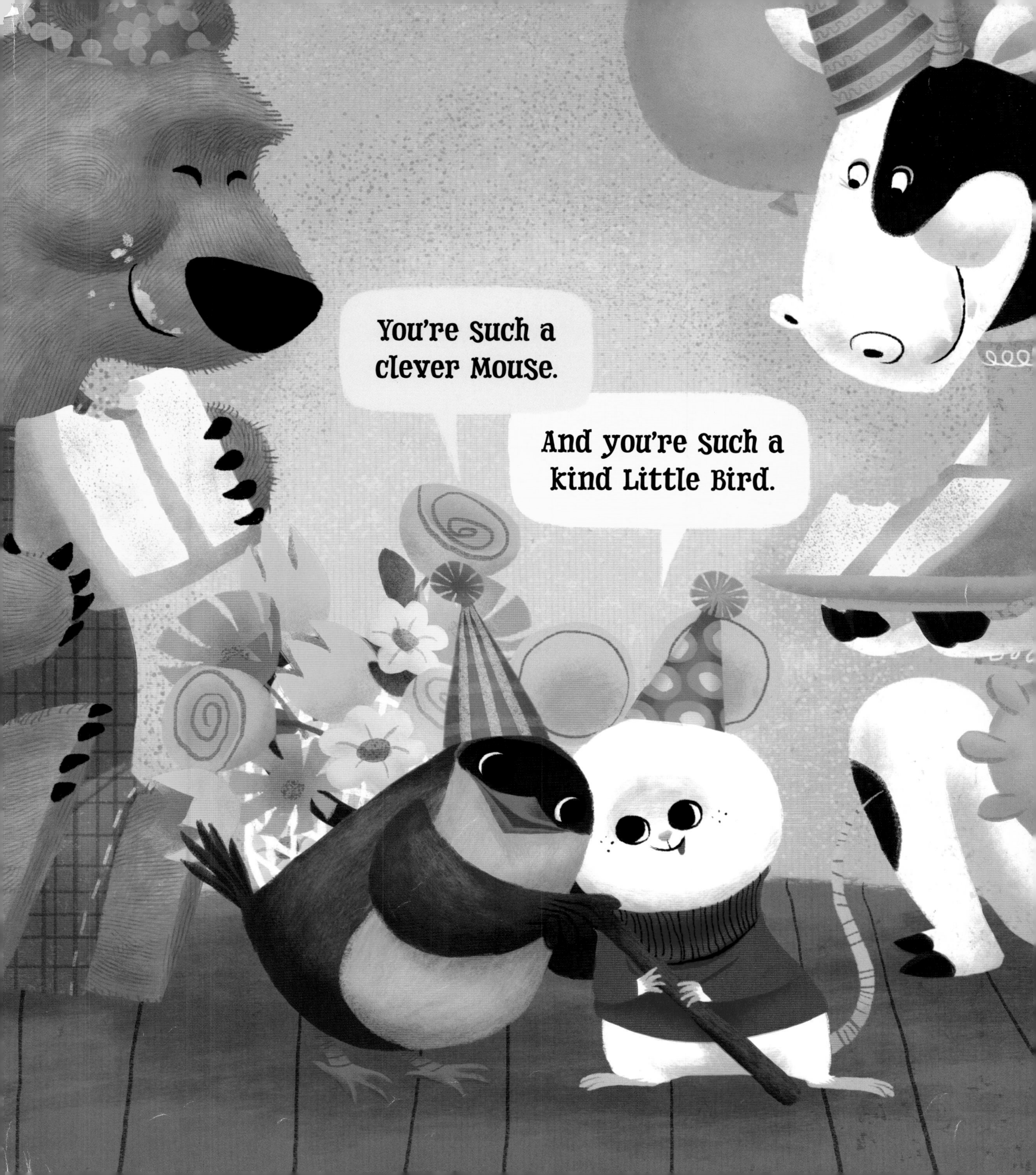
You're such a clever Mouse.
And you're such a kind Little Bird.

Copyright © 2014 by LeUyen Pham

All rights reserved.

Manufactured in China.

No part of this book may be used or reproduced in any manner whatsoever
without written permission except in the case of brief quotations embodied
in critical articles and reviews.

For information address HarperCollins Children's Books, a division of
HarperCollins Publishers, 10 East 53rd Street, New York, NY 10022.
www.harpercollinschildrens.com

Library of Congress Cataloging-in-Publication Data

ISBN 978-0-06-199264-3 (trade bdg.)

The illustrations for this book were rendered in pencil and colored digitally.

Typography by Dana Fritts and LeUyen Pham

14 15 16 17 18   SCP   10 9 8 7 6 5 4 3 2 1

❖

First Edition

For Mike and Chris,
who helped me make the cake,
and for Adrien,
who gets to eat it